PANI

To:
Daddy,
My Super-
hero! I Love
you!
Onyx

Acknowledgements

First, I would like to thank God who is and always will be the head of my life.

My best friend Joy for being there with me every step of the way. Joy I cannot even begin to tell you how much you mean to me.

My fiancé Keith this has been a very rocky ride thank you for continuing to love me.
What can I say about my Pastor Kenneth Jones Jr.? You have not only been my Pastor, but you have been my counselor, protector and friend. You and First Lady Dana are models for Keith and I. Thank you for ALL that you do.

Last, but certainly not least. Minister Ella Burton when I grow up, I want to be just
like you!!

Ok everyone. Let's go!!

-Onyx

Chapter 1

The bright shining sun woke me up out of a fit filled
sleep. The first thing that I notice before I even open my eyes is the fact that my throat is very scratchy. I am a singer, so I hope that I can fix this. Let me get up out of this bed, so that I can make me some tea. As I began to walk down
the stairs toward the kitchen it was like my breath was snatched away with every step that I took. I had to sit down on the bottom step for like 10 minutes just to get myself together enough to walk into the kitchen I walked into the kitchen to put on a pot of tea. I rest my hands on the edge of the sink. I have never been so exhausted in my whole life, and I just

woke up! I make my tea, and slowly begin to pull myself back up the stairs. My best friend lives in Michigan. I speak to her on the phone several times a day. When I got back to the top of the stairs, I took out my phone to give Joy a call. The phone barely rang 2 times before she answered. The first sentence out of her mouth is," Onyx, you need to go to the hospital." I had been sick quite a few times, but to be honest with everyone including myself I had never felt this way. I actually felt like I was drowning, and I was not even near any water. Tears slowly rolled down my cheeks. I did not really know what was wrong with me. I just knew that it was pretty bad. Worse than I had ever experienced before. During this whole morning the only constant I can remember doing is calling on the name of Jesus. I knew that everything had to bow to the name of Jesus. Even this horrible sickness. I couldn't even begin to wrap my mind around the possibility that I could possibly have that dreaded disease that is killing everybody. I can't take my temperature, because I don't have a thermometer. There wasn't a thermometer to be had in the entire town. This was crazy, as I am a manager at one of the largest retails stores in our country. I have toilet paper, Lysol spray, Lysol wipes and even hand sanitizer, but no thermometer. To be straight up I honestly did not think this stuff was real anyway. I thought it was something made up by our government. I mean the only people that I ever saw on TV, or in papers to get the virus were some famous people with no symptoms. The Map Virus doesn't really exist does it? They are just trying to scare everyone. I must admit it is working on me. I am scared. I can't believe that I can't breathe.

Chapter 2

The uber driver took one look at me and said, "I hope you don't have that Map Virus crap!" I slammed the door and just laid back in my seat. I honestly didn't know. I mean I had been doing everything that everyone told me to do, but I still didn't really know. I had been holding my breath for 10 seconds every morning, and today was the first day that simple test had been hard. While the driver sped down the street, I just lay there watching the trees go by. Sooner rather than later we pulled up to the emergency room. I closed my eyes and took as big a breath that I could and got out of the car. I said a little prayer half-heartedly and walked in the doors.

They had a little station between the doors where they took your temperature and handed you a mask. My temperature was 102.8. I slumped down in a wheelchair, and the nurse just wheeled me in the back. For the first time that entire day I was truly afraid. I was afraid that I was not going to make it out of this hospital. I tried to think of the fancy prayers that I had heard
in my life, and I couldn't remember a single one. I could not remember, a book, chapter or verse of any scripture. Not even the 23rd or 91st Number of Psalms. I just began to talk to Jesus with my heart. I did not know any proper words, but for the time it felt like I could literally feel him holding my hand. In my mind I could feel the melody of Yes, Jesus Loves Me. It was playing over and over in my head. Yes, I was very sick, and did not know that I was in this world, but I did know that Jesus loved

me. Yep He loved me. Even after all the wrong that I had done in my whole miserable life. After all the lies that I had told, all the dope I had smoked. He still loved my pitiful self. I had a high fever. I could barely breathe. My heart was racing, but I knew in my heart that Jesus loved me. The next thing I knew was that I was in La-La land. The melody to that little song had rocked me to sleep. I could feel myself coming to, but I still felt like someone was sitting on my chest. Where was I? I had no idea. I just knew that I was about to die. I could hear beeping noises off in the distance. I had never been so afraid in all my life. I was literally struggling for every breath that I took. My body felt like it was on fire. Yet I could not open my eyes. I could not wake up. Is this what dying felt like? Even though I felt all of these scary things it was like I could feel someone's arms wrapped tightly around me whispering in my ear that no matter how bad things got I was going to be ok. I would live and not die. Before I knew what was happening, I lapsed back into a deep sleep. It was like finally I had settled into taking shallow breaths. Was this how life was going to be for me? Learning to breathe like I was breathing through a straw?

Chapter 3

It was like my life was flashing before my closed eyelids like a movie. All the good that I had done, and all the bad too. It showed me a scene before I got sick. There was a lady going through my grocery line in a full-length mink coat. She was attempting to buy 2 packages of chicken. Then there was a lady behind her with food stamps. She too was attempting to buy 2 packages of chicken. I had to tell them both that they could only buy one. This disease is affecting everybody! It does not matter if you are black, or white. Rich, or poor! Everyone was affected by this pandemic. This movie was kind of weird, because then I could see me in my late teens walking down the aisle towards my first husband. I was a bride, and I thought that this was the happiest day of my life. I was in a small church. My future Sister-In-Law had let me borrow this little cute white dress, and even the veil on my head! The saying goes something borrowed huh. Well this entire outfit is borrowed! At least I got that part right. I am very happy. I look towards the front of the church. My soon to be husband looks like he is happy as well. The girl standing at the altar. Who was she? Borrowed too, I guess! I look at my soon to be husband, and his features changed right in front of me! He looked like the devil himself, but before I could turn around and run, my mind flashed to a different scene in my head. This time I was sitting on the floor in front of a gas heater with a piece of a car antenna hanging out of my mouth. I kept heating the tip of it with a lighter. It was getting pretty hot burning my lips even. I still did not let that antenna go. Why did I keep flicking that lighter in front of that gas? Heater? Didn't I know that I could blow myself up? The fact truthfully was that I didn't care. Where was my husband? Where were my kids? I did have some didn't I? What in the world was? I doing? Why was I smoking crack? That was what I was doing. What was that awful…? Wait a minute! Look at my face! I could see my reflection in the cracked mirror in front of me, and I looked completely blissful. Like I did not have a care in the world. As long as I had that piece of antenna, that lighter, and that little pile of little yellow rocks in front of me. Aw shoot. Here comes another scene shift. I am holding onto a walker. I am in a bank I guess, because I am handing the teller a note. She takes a look at the note, and the blood drains from her face. All of a sudden, she is stuffing wads of money in my purse.

Hey! I'm robbing this bank on a walker! With a note too! I need to see that note! I want to read what it said, but before I could ask her to give back the note, she shoves it down into my purse with the wads of money. I politely thank the lady and turn around and walk out the door! The security guard even held the door for me as I left. I had asked this girl to give me a ride to the bank to cash my check. Yet I had just robbed the bank, and walked back to her car, got in, and she calmly rode away. She was the getaway driver for a bank robbery, and she didn't even know it!

Chapter 4

The next scene began to play. I could see myself laying naked on the floor of a cell. I could literally hear myself crying out to God," If you are up there, and I don't know for sure that you are. Save me!" The God that I serve now showed up and showed out! Gave me a peace that surpassed all of MY understanding. I had always thought I was worth less than nothing. That I meant nothing to anybody, but at that moment I knew that I meant something to Jesus. It didn't matter anymore what others thought. I knew without a shadow of a doubt that Jesus loved me!

On to the next scene. Sitting in the back of a church, and the choir is throwing down! I look down at my clothes. They aren't regular church clothes. Just old pants and a shirt. I want to jump up, but as I look around, I notice that others are staring at me already! Before I get to wonder anymore the screen jumps again. This time I am in the choir singing at the top of my lungs just praising God! I love it! I look up at the video monitor, and notice that I'm even wearing church clothes now! I look beautiful! My head is thrown back, and I am singing at the top of my lungs! As our song came to a close my Pastor got out of his chair and began preaching his heart out! This time when the scene changed, I wanted to yell out, "NO! Wait!" When this scene opens a very light skinned man is sitting across from me in a uniform no less! With blue-green eyes, and a gray goatee. Man, he is handsome! He had a velvety baritone voice that sent chills up my spine. He looks very interested in me. In ME?? Can you believe it?? I sure couldn't. Nobody that handsome had ever been interested in someone like me. Who am I kidding. I had through much too much. Even if this handsome man was interested in me, I wasn't interested in him! Not for real anyway. I was going to be single the rest of my life. Look man, let me be honest with you. I have had a pretty messed up life. I am not looking for a one-night stand. "Well pretty lady, I am not looking for a one-night stand either. I am looking for a queen to make my wife." I dropped my fork. Aw man the scene changed again. That was getting good! This time I am sitting at a table next to that handsome light skinned man listening to my Pastor break down Romans 8:28-And we know that all things work together for the good of those who love the Lord and are called according to His purpose. Now this means it doesn't matter if things are good in your eyes, or bad. They all work together for our good. That was pretty deep for me. I had been through so much bad in my life, and now I know that it's going to work together for my good. I look over to the handsome light skinned guy with the blue-green eyes. How is he going to work together?

For my good?

He reaches for my hand. Oh my goodness! We are a couple! Now somebody please tell me how this is going to work together for my good?

Chapter 5

I'm getting tired of this movie garbage.
What am I doing in a Bridal Shop?
Ringing a bell, no less! Oh my! I'm
getting married!? I feel at peace about it
too. I'm really happy about getting
married. Oh, my goodness. What is that
beeping noise? What happened to the
movie that has been? Playing in my
head? Where am I? Is the beeping in
heaven? How come I can't open my
eyes? What's happening right now? "Ms.
King? Ms. King? Can you hear me? I
need you to open your eyes if you can.
I'm Dr. Anul. You're at Heathrow
Hospital. You have the Map Virus. You
have been on a ventilator for 5 days. I've

had you in an induced coma. I wanted you to rest. Your lungs had been working so hard for so long. You really needed to rest." Map Virus? Please don't tell me that I caught that awful disease that has been killing people the last couple of months. "Well I hate to be the bearer of bad news, but you and your boyfriend caught it. He is in the room just down the hall." Now I know that I had to be still dreaming. I had the Map Virus, and my boyfriend does too?? How did we get it? Why did we get it? Then my mind went back to that Bible Study that my pastor had taught using Romans 8:28. All things were going to work out for my good according to His purpose. Even this dreaded Corona Virus that me, and my boyfriend caught. How God was going to make this work out for my good I really didn't know. What I did know was that this was hard. I mean this disease was killing people! There was no cure. No one knew anything about it except that it was airborne. That it attacks your lungs and causes severe respiratory issues. It seemed like the entire nation had come to a screeching halt. They had the TV going in my room to keep me company, I guess. They didn't know that I had never been a TV person. I loved reading and music best. Now that I was awake, I hoped they brought me something to read. I needed something to read.

I was not going to just lay here, and just give in to this disease. I refused to lay here and die. As soon as that thought crossed my mind, I became aware of the moans around me, and mostly the horrible silence. There was such suffering around me. Father God in the name of Jesus please heal these sick people. Whether it is in this world or the next. Just end all of their suffering. Not being able to breathe was bad enough, but coupled with the upper back, and chest pain, and it's almost unbearable.

What I found helpful for me was to pray for those around me. "Excuse me ma'am." I turned my head towards the door of my hospital room, and there stood this young masked lady no more than 30 years old. She had tears streaming down her face. My heart just began to melt for her. She looked so pained.

Chapter 6

" I don't mean to bother you, but I need to get this off me before I leave this place to go home to my husband and babies. This is so hard. People are so sick. I'm trying to be their nurse, counselor and missing family members. These people are dying. I don't even begin to know how to help them. Shoot the doctors don't even know. " She dropped down in the chair next to my bed with tear-soaked eyes. I closed my eyes to send up a quick prayer. Lord please move me out of the way. Give me the words to say to this child.

In a soft voice I said baby just your mere presence is helping. Showing that beautiful smile helps more than you know. Do you know how scary it is to have a disease that even the doctors don't haven't dealt with? Understand. It is scary and it is lonely. " But… How do you deal with it? You're sick too." Yes baby I am, but if I dwelt on that I would be miserable as all get out! I keep my mind and prayers on everybody else. Especially the doctors. They have to feel absolutely helpless. They are trying everything that they know, and yet people are still dying. Think about that. When they first decided to go to medical school, they were all gung-ho to help people. Sure, there are instances where they do not have a cure like cancer and sickle cell, but at least they know how to treat the symptoms without making them worse. Well with this Map Virus they have no idea what to expect. They are actually figuring out what Christian's have known all along. They are just practicing medicine. Most of them are coming face to face with that God complex that they all have. It has to really be killing them to learn that they aren't gods after all. Just mere men with a small amount of knowledge. Everyone is coming to the fact that they need the one true God to be able to survive. So, in fact everyone honestly needs God, and what I am constantly praying for is that everyone begins to accept this. Baby you just keep taking care of people with compassion in your heart, and believe me God is going to turn things around. Make sure that even when you leave work that you continue to mask up and wear gloves. Practice social distancing. I do not think things will ever go back to the way they were. We are going to have a new normal. I honestly believe more people than ever are going to turn towards the Lord. They simply are not going to have a choice. He is the only one who can save us now. As she stood up to leave, she smiled down at me shyly. "Thank you for talking to me. I feel so much better now." Baby I'm glad that I could help. You have no idea how much helping you helped me! Just spending this little time talking to you about your problems helped me not concentrate on my own. This world is not going to get any better. Only worse. We have to catch a little bit of peace wherever we can.

Chapter 7

I slept well that night. No pain or nothing. I woke up feeling really refreshed the next morning. I felt better than I have in a long time. I know last night that young lady thought our little conversation was solely for her benefit, but it was for me as well. I had a whole new attitude today. I couldn't wait until that doctor came to see me today. I got out of the bed for the first time since I had been in that hospital. See another thing about COVID-19 is that it saps your energy. I mean it really wipes you out!! When I talk about the symptoms that I had let me be very clear about them. The coughing, aching, fever and chills, energy zapping was not like anyone had ever experienced. It was constant! Severe times 10! Anyway, I jumped out of that bed on my own and walked into that bathroom and washed up my body all by myself. I went back to my room, and slowly began to walk the perimeter. You see my wind was totally taken away from me. I knew that I had to try to strengthen my lungs. Walking slowly around that room was the best way that I could do that at the time. It was very hard, but I knew that even though I could not have any visitors. My Father in heaven who was the only visitor who mattered anyway had been there with me all the time. He would give me the strength to walk around that room. See, my Word told me that his strength was perfect. That He would carry us when we couldn't go on. I just began to talk to Him. With every step I took. I reminded God of His promises to me that He gave me in His Word. I could not for the life of me remember the addresses, but I remembered the promises. I knew that God was holy, and could not lie, so I simply prefaced each step and each promise with you said…. Before I knew it, I had walked a whole hour. Just talking to God. The next thing I knew my doctor walked in the room." How are you doing today Ms. King? Looks like you are feeling pretty good. "

Doctor, I am feeling really good today. Better than I have since this whole thing started. I am walking around now trying to build my strength back up. Trying together my breathing better.

"Wonderful! Come sit down so that I can check your oxygen and listen to your chest. I think we are heading in the right direction. We will have you back home in no time." I gingerly stood up to continue my walk around my room. Just smiling to myself. See the doctor did not know who my main physician was. The song "Never Would Have Made It" just began to play over and over in my mind. I was going to make it out of here. The doctor was not sure, the nursing staff was not sure. For the first time I was sure. It came to me clear as a bell. My fiancé was upstairs in ICU. I had not even prayed for him before now. I thought it would be selfish. I forgot about his children. He was a twin. I forgot about his twin. Not only did I not think about his twin. I did not think about his other siblings either. I was not the only one who loved him and needed him. The fact that I did not think about them was selfish in itself. I stopped right in my tracks and bowed my head. Father God in the name of Jesus. First, I just want to say thank you for being God all by yourself. Thank you for this hospital. Thank you for this hospital staff. Thank you for my healing. I thank you for taking care of my family and friends. I thank you for bringing your Word back to my remembrance. Now Lord I want to thank you for Keith. I want to thank you for allowing him to show me what real love is. Father, he is upstairs fighting for his life. I never came to you about this before, because I did not want to seem selfish. It was selfish for me not to. Lord Jesus clear his lungs. His very own breath is not enough to sustain him right now. Give him your breath. Please let the medicine work. Lord please take that Map Virus away from his body. I know that he is in pain, and I ask that you remove that horrible pain, or at least give him the strength to bear it. Heal him Father. I need him so. I dropped to my knees the feelings of fear that I had just overtook me like a wave, but I knew that God could heal him. He had healed me. No, the doctors had not said it yet, but I knew all the same. Since

He had healed me, I knew that He could heal Keith.

Chapter 8

I didn't know a special way to pray. I just spoke to God directly from my heart. Somehow, I knew that it was good enough. Nobody had told me. I just knew. See, being in that hospital was hard. It was extremely lonely. When I was in ICU, and didn't know if I was in this world, or the next. It didn't matter I guess, but now that I was awake, I was suddenly aware that I was extremely lonely. The one person who I would have done anything to have a visit from was upstairs fighting for his life. For the first time it dawned on me that I had started to think of us as an us. I didn't want to lose him. I loved him. God had given him to me. He was far from perfect, but so was I. We were planning our wedding for goodness sake. "Ms. King, you have been walking around this room for 3 days now. How about we take it out to the hallway?" I looked over at my door, and there stood my nurse in that hazmat gear. I knew they had to wear it, but it still cracked me up when I saw it. Yes, ma'am I'm ready to take my walking to the hallway. I'm feeling much better today. " Okay. Put this mask on, and this gown in the back first." I was so excited. I was tired of looking at the 4 walls in that hospital room. That first walk out in the hallway was like I was walking in another world. It was then when I noticed how cut off from the world I really was. At the end of the hallway was a closed door with a little glass window towards the top of it. It was then that I also realized how seriously afraid of people like me the world was. What I didn't know was this was just the beginning of the prejudice that I would face before this was all over.

It felt so good to be walking in that little hallway. I knew that soon I was going to be getting out of the hospital. I just had to continue building my strength. The nurse continued to push food at me telling me that it would give me strength. What they didn't understand was that I couldn't smell, or taste anything. I no longer lived to eat food. Now I am a big girl, so food is something that I love, but now it wasn't fun to eat. I had to make myself swallow every mouthful.

Chapter 9

"Alright. Ms. King are you ready to go home today? Can you get a ride? Or do you need us to provide you with one?" I couldn't believe it! I was really going home! I knew that this day was coming, but I didn't think it was coming so soon. I have been here 8 days! I reached for my phone to text Keith. He couldn't talk back to me, but we kept in constant contact with each other that way. I had asked the ICU nurses to keep his phone charged, and in his hand. They were kind enough to do it too. We may not have been able to talk to each other face to face, but we kept in touch with each other, and everything that was happening with each other. I used my thumbs and couldn't text fast enough. I was so excited to be going home. I called my ride right away. I wasn't even paying attention to the rest of what the doctor was saying. I had to slow him down and have him start over. Doctor I was really excited, and honestly didn't hear what you said."Lol. It's ok Ms. King. I just said that your oxygen level has steadily been above 96. Even when you're up and moving, therefore I am comfortable sending you home. Can you have a ride here at 2pm?" I could hardly contain my excitement. I just began thanking God for his healing right then. I had been so sick when I came through those hospital doors. Then when I began to think about them diagnosing me as having the Map Virus, I praised Him all the more. I had been diagnosed with a deadly virus that was stripping me of my very breath. The doctors and scientists had no idea of what it was let alone have a cure for it, but I knew the great physician. He knew when I walked through those doors that I was going to walk out of them again. I thought about so many who had lost their battle. I even thought about those still fighting the battle and began to praise Him all the more. I was simply humbled that God saw fit to heal me. ME. I was worth nothing. An ex junkie, Excon, an ex any and everything that you could think of, and God saw fit to hear little old me. I was just praising Him with tears rolling down my face. The doctor was just watching me like I had lost my mind, but he didn't understand. To actually, be healed of something that people were dying from every day. Something that even he had no idea how to cure. So that I knew without a shadow of a doubt that it was God Himself that had healed my physical body. It was absolutely mind blowing. He told me that the nurse would be in with discharge papers soon.

Chapter 10

On my ride home I really could not believe I had been there 8 days. I knew that I had to quarantine myself for 14 days, but I was going home. I would do anything! I was told to be sure and include alkaline in my diet daily. I had looked at the nurse quizzically and she then explained that lemons have alkaline in them, and that they kill the virus on contact. I had to continue doing as much exercise as my body would take to continue to strengthen my lungs. My senses of taste and smell were completely gone, but I had to eat to keep building my strength. What was honestly troubling me was the fact that I was leaving my fiancé there, and wasn't sure if he was going to be coming home to me at all. He was still so very sick. Worrying about him was going to help me keep my mind off of myself. I wonder what he is doing right now. I love him so much. It was a beautiful day. Just perfect for my home going. God saw fit for me to leave this miserable hospital. I am healed y'all! I'm healed! From the top of my head to the soles of my feet...We pulled up to the store, so that I could use the pharmacy to get my medicine. Yes, I had been healed, but I must remember that God also heals through medicine, so I was going to get and take this medicine. As I am looking all around me. I noticed that hardly no one was wearing a mask. I thought back to how sick I was and just slowly shook my head. It was so sad. I began looking at all the senior citizens and children and actually cringing knowing how horrible the Map Virus was. It was like they were all playing with a very hot stove. Don't they know that they will get burned. This disease is nothing to play with at all! As me and my Papa walked into the store, I started to feel self-conscious about my appearance. Then it dawned on me. I had just fought the dreaded Map Virus and WON!! I had nothing to feel self-conscious about. I don't care how I looked. On the inside I was standing 8 feet tall. I seemed like everyone around me was staring at me. Walking away from me like I was a leper. Wait a minute. I'm not contagious anymore! I felt like I was yelling, but I was yelling in my mind. It was like people were walking to a whole other aisle just to get away from me. What is going on? I just walked to the pharmacy window. I just wanted to go home. "Hey are you ok? You're mighty quiet over there. Are you glad to be going home? I know I hate hospitals." I look over at my Papa and just smile. I love my Papa so much. He wasn't my biological father, but I couldn't love him anymore if he was. Yes papa. I am glad to be going home. Just thinking how all of this seemed like a dream. It doesn't seem like I have been in the hospital at all. It seemed so weird to be going home without Keith. I can't help, but to worry about him. I look out the window, and softly say. God please heal his body.

Chapter 11

I unlock the door and slowly walk inside.
I put the cold food in the refrigerator and
made my way upstairs to bed. I was
exhausted. It took a lot of energy just
coming home. Yeah, I did stop at
the store but dang! I lay across the bed
just to rest a bit, but I didn't wake up
until the next morning. I was stiff and
noticed that it was deathly silent. Before
I even sat up, I had a little talk with my
Daddy. Father in heaven, thank you for
this day. Thank you for waking me up
this morning and starting me on my way.
Thank you for healing my body of that

horrible disease. I am thanking you in advance for healing Keith. Help me to not fear being alone and protect me from my own negative thoughts. The nurse had told me how the alkaline found in lemons would kill the virus. I still had no taste or smell. I would just put an entire wedge in my tea. That will be the only proof that I'm even taking the lemon. My next 2 weeks flew by in a blur. I slept most of the time. My strength was almost gone. It's taking me quite a while to get it back. The nurse in the hospital had told me that I had to eat to get my strength built back up. It's been 2 weeks, and my sense of taste and smell had not come back. I'm tired of eating to a timer. Right before going into the hospital I had moved into Keith's duplex. We were trying to save money for our wedding. Going up and down the stairs was really helping in giving me strength. I had concentrated on giving the house a good disinfecting before Keith came back home. In the pit of my stomach and in the back of my mind I thought he wasn't going to come home. I thought Keith was going to die honestly. I knew that God had the power to heal Keith. I just didn't think He would. I tried not to think about living a life without Keith, but in my mind, I knew that was exactly what it boiled down to. I just tried to keep my mind on getting better. Slowly, but surely my sense of smell was coming back, and I began eating everything in sight! I ate all the time! It was like I had a tape worm, but not only was I am eating all the time I was constantly in a state of anxiousness. It was like I had a hyper sense of awareness. I made sure, to always be upstairs by 10pm. Then I just lay awake listening for strange noises in the night. Finally, around 3:30-4am I would fall off to sleep. I would call my friend Joy in the middle of the night. She always answered the phone. She knew that I was just paranoid, yet she still answered the phone every time I called. Stupid conversations, or not. She answered every time, she really was my best friend. I loved her so very much. She has been my best friend for almost 30 years. It truly was a blessing.

Chapter 12

The hospital just called me. I have to have home oxygen set up before Keith can come home. Thank you, Jesus, He is coming home! Oh, praise the Lord! I was so afraid that he wasn't going to come out of this. Well he did, and now he was coming home. I am so glad that we had made the decision to move in together before all of this madness happened. Somebody had to get this house ready for him to come home to. You know most people talk a good game, but when it comes time for them to put up, they usually back down. I am so glad that I am here to take care of him. He can be a bit much at times, but he is mine, and I can and will take care of him. Oh, that's my door! They must be here to set up the oxygen. I open the door, but do not see anyone, I look up because I hear someone calling my name."Ms. King! Ms. King! I need you to step back in your house. Close the door, and I will leave your machines on the porch. Then I will call you and tell you how to set it up. This is what we call a contactless delivery... I am not supposed to have any contact with you. Go back in your house!" Ok another bout with discrimination as far as the Map Virus is concerned. Doesn't he understand that I am out of the hospital now. I am not sick anymore! I can't give him the CMap Virus! I do not have it anymore! I step back into the house and slam the door. I grab my phone to wait for him to call. After about 5 minutes he does. He tells me to bring the equipment inside.

Then he tells me how to set it up. I drag the larger machine upstairs to Keith's bedroom. I had changed his bedding. Totally disinfected his bedroom. I had purchased an air mattress for the other room. I had set up camp there for myself. I could tell already how everyone would be afraid of him. Everyone seemed so concerned, but I knew that no one would be willing to help him like he needed to be helped, so I would help him myself. I didn't care what anyone thought about us living together now. We needed each other. Since both of us had contracted the Map Virus the rules had changed. We needed each other. For the first time the quote me and you against the world has taken on a whole new meaning. When he came home, he is really going to see that it truly is him and I against the world. I closed the door to his bedroom and made my way across the hall to my makeshift room. I loved him so much. I was leery about how the nurses were taking care of him at the hospital. It would literally drive me crazy to think about him here all alone trying to take care of himself while oxygen dependent. It was hard enough for me to take care of myself, and I wasn't oxygen dependent. I could not even imagine the man that I loved trying to do it leaning on an oxygen pole. I had to drink a cup of tea with a lemon wedge in it every day. Then I sipped on water with fresh lemon all day long. I knew that it had been keeping the virus away from me, and I had to make sure Keith drank that as well. I was going to take care of my man, myself. I would make sure he had fresh lemon every day.

Chapter 13

Ok. There are fresh linens on his bed Pajamas are laid across the foot of his bed. His oxygen machine is on and set to the right number. All he had to do is put it on. The ambulance bringing him home would be here any minute. They had left the hospital 30 minutes ago. Oh, I hear them pulling up in the back. My honey is home!! Oh, I have been so lonely! I have worried about him so bad. Now that he was home at least I would be sure, that he is well taken care of. "Hi honey! I'm home." I turned my head away to prevent tears from falling down my face. I was standing in the doorway while the ambulance drivers were helping him off the gurneys. See they weren't allowed to come into our home. Everyone was so paranoid. The world was so paranoid. The world was so afraid of catching the dreaded Map Virus. If they knew that you had had it, they were afraid of you which didn't make any sense to me. Since I had the dreaded Virus and beat it. So many others were not so fortunate. Whatever was in my blood could cure them if they ever caught it. That just further let me know that moving in with Keith was the best decision that I could make for the two of us. People were really afraid of this Virus. I honestly could not blame them. I mean people were dying. I never in my life thought something like this could happen. No one had been there for me, but I was going to be there for him. I'm sure that I am going to find things about him that I don't like just like he is going to find things about me that he doesn't like. I am really nervous about this. I have never in my life trusted someone like this. Yes, there were some good people in this world, but there are monsters in this world. Most people didn't know this. I always had, but I didn't want them to hurt him. I loved him too much. When I came home from the hospital it was so hard. I had to take care of myself. I didn't want him to have to go through what I did. I had hurt enough for everyone in my life. I know in the past that we had said it's me and him against the world, but it really is. It's me and him against this whole world.

Chapter 14

As I lay on this very comfortable air mattress (if I say so myself) I am content. I had settled into a routine as far as taking care of Keith. I was finished with my 14 days of quarantine. We had decided that Keith would spend his 14 days quarantine in the master bedroom and bath. I would bring his meals and medications on a tray to his door. We would always be masked while in each other's presence. He was worried about re-infecting me, but I wasn't afraid of him. I loved him and would take care of him until he was able to take care of himself. He had lost so much weight. That's ok. When I agreed to marry him, I knew that this might someday be a part of it. Now don't get me wrong. I didn't think it would be happening before I could even get down the aisle, but oh well. I love this man. God gave him to me. I am going to cherish him for the rest of my days. He is going to sleep quite a bit for the next 2 weeks, but I will make sure that he eats and gets his medication. I get to spend some much-needed time in the Word. I guess I need to go to the grocery store tomorrow to make sure that we have everything that we need. I lay back and finally take a breath, happy that we were both under the same roof. Keith was no longer in the hospital. I didn't have to worry about getting a good night's sleep tonight. I decide to go to the store that I work at to get the things that we need. My store is small, and I know where things are. Plus, I am going back to work there as soon as I get 2 negative tests. This Map Virus has been so hard. I do understand why I have to have 2 negative tests before I go back to work since I worked in a grocery store. I couldn't wait to go back just to see the store. Was I nervous? Yes. Excited at the same time. I jumped up and began to write my grocery list. Trying to figure out things that he will eat is blowing my mind. I know that he won't have an appetite for at least 2 weeks. I'm going to sure try though.

Chapter 15

I felt really good walking into the store until I began to see people that I knew. They began to go to a completely different aisle when they saw me coming. At first, I thought it was isolated incidents until it happened all the way through the store. To put the cherry on top of the cake when I got to the register after I got all my things on the belt the cashier took one long look at me and walked away from the register! At first, I just stood there with my mouth wide open. I could not believe that she actually did that! I am a Manager and knew exactly who she was, also, I was for sure going to contact corporate, and file a complaint. I turned around and the Customer Service Manager was right there so I say, "Hey should I leave and go somewhere else?" She just shrugs and says, "I would" So, I just leave the groceries on the belt, and walk out. I was so upset. Now I know what lepers feel like. Just the stigma of having the Map Virus was horrible. I thought things were going to be so much better since I had made it out of the hospital, but that just wasn't true. It seemed like people would have been happier had I just died. That way the Map Virus could remain that mystical disease that would kill you. Well that is not what happened. God had healed me. My fiancé too. Praise God we had beat the Map Virus. As I walked out to my car that was exactly what was going through my mind. I wasn't upset at all. Now I was going to call corporate and complain about the horrible service I received today. Yes, I absolutely am, but I am not upset. This Map Virus is killing people, so I understand the fear. Now while I understood the fear. I am still human, and my feelings were definitely hurt. I am definitely thankful to God for having Keith in my life. I could imagine how my life would be if Keith was afraid of me, or I was afraid of him. It has made us so very close. Even though he is still pretty sick he will get better every day. I don't know the reason yet, but there is really something amazing that God has for us to do. Us catching the Map Virus was preparing us for something huge. I am so very excited to find out what it is. The love I have for my Father in heaven is just so amazing. I mean yeah when I was laying on that hospital bed drowning in my own mucus with the doctor standing next to my bed not knowing what to do to save me, I had wasn't sure whether I was going to be healed on this side or the next, but I was sure that God was going to heal me. God was also with the man that was going to be my husband as he went through his own battle with the Map Virus. It just really blew my mind how much God loved me. If I had ever doubted it in my life before I didn't now. This whole thing has been so very, very scary. So many people have lost their lives. Yet I am still here. I no longer feel as though I have a choice in whether, or not my soul will say yes. My soul not only says yes but is yes!! My soul has been lifted in ways I couldn't even imagine. I just know that I intend to spend the rest of my life running for my Lord and Savior Jesus Christ.

Chapter 16

Life for me is beginning to settle down. I can hear Keith beginning to move around more. I hear his oxygen machine and know that he is doing better. I can tell by his food trays. His appetite is picking back up. God is really blessing me in so many ways. I find myself spending more and more time in my Word. Thinking about the many God-fearing women that God has placed in my life. Thinking about the Bible teaching and Bible preaching church that I have been blessed to be a part of. I have grown leaps and bounds. So much so that I can actually look at my catching the Map Virus as an opportunity to tell of God's amazing grace. God never puts more on us than we can bear. So, He knew that I could bear being infected with that deadly Virus. He knew from the beginning that He was going to heal me. Nothing catches God by surprise. He knew all along that He was going to heal Keith. I was afraid for no reason at all. I should have known. No matter what I had ever done it was never about me. Not my catching the Map Virus, or me getting healed from the Map Virus. None of it was about me. It was all just an opportunity for God to show His power, to show His love toward us. "Onyx" I turned around and looked up startled at Keith standing in the doorway with his mask on. "Can I have a snack?" I almost break down and start crying. He has lost so much weight, but I love him so very much. God has truly healed his body. Yes, honey absolutely. Would you like something special? I try to make sure that we have all the foods he likes. He turns around and walks back to his room. Tears were streaming down my face as I reached for my mask to go down and make him a snack. We decided to continue to be masked up until he was no longer in quarantine. We still didn't want me to be re-infected. I love him so very much. I am just so grateful for his healing. I am tingling with excitement. I look down at what I have prepared. It looks like something that I would have prepared for a child., but I am truly grateful that he is requesting anything extra to eat at all. He has basically been nibbling at the things I have been putting on his tray like a little mouse when he is a full-grown man.

I know that sometimes we can get pretty upset about the things in our lives, but we have got to really begin being grateful for even the little things in life that we have constantly taken for granted.

Yes, I know that it is easier said than done, and that's why I say there are some things that we need to begin working on. We will never be able to do it until we at least begin. Everyone has to start somewhere. I guess I'd better get this food up to him before he changes his mind about eating it at all. That would be downright awful.

Chapter 17

The company that I work for is supposed to pay me for time off from work for testing positive for the Map Virus then put me on short term disability to pay me something until I can come back to work. Mortgage companies, utility companies and car loan companies are waiving late fees for the next couple months, but the sad thing about all that is, they are just pushing back when things are due. Then they are going to make them all due at once, and so many people are going to be in dire straits.

My company has yet to pay me at all. Acting like they aren't aware of the things that are going on. Believe me. They are aware. It just doesn't affect them, so they don't care. My company says all over the TV that they are doing so much to help employees who become infected with the Map Virus, and it is simply not true. Man cannot depend on man to save him during this time. Man has got to solely trust and depend on God. God is the only thing that is going to see us through this horrible time. Man can and will let you down every time. I just feel like so many need to know that right now. Times are hard out here, and God is the only thing that can see us through. It's funny how it took something this drastic to make us aware of what men and women of God have been saying to us for decades. Why do we realize that God is all we need?
When God is all we have? I guess we ought to just really be glad that God is

not like us. We really ought to be glad that God is loving and forgiving. As I go back to my room it dawns on me how I have not been lonely. I mean yeah Keith is here now to keep me company, but even before he came home for me to take care of, I was simply not lonely. There have been so many people dealing with mental health issues. Mainly depression. Even children who aren't able to attend school right now are severely depressed. School for them is not only a place of learning, but they got to relieve their social anxieties there as well. Now they are stuck in their houses with their immediate families going to school online. What about family members dealing with abuse?

They are literally trapped in their houses with their abusers. I lay in here on my bed worrying about so many things. How can I worry about? things I have no control over. I guess I need to go back to the way I was when I was in the hospital. Not only keeping my mind off myself, but also, off other problems who I couldn't solve. Turning it over to Jesus and letting Him work it out. The Map Virus and its issues are much too much for me to deal with. I am going to allow my Father In heaven the creator of all things including the outcome of the pandemic to work it out!

Chapter 18

Keith is finally off quarantine. We have
settled into a pretty good routine. Neither
of us are employed right now, and I
know that even that is a part of God's
divine plan. Waiting on strangers for
handouts, and unemployment is
something that is totally foreign to me.
Trying not to worry about even where
our next meal is going to come from is
just something that I am not prepared to
do. I now know and believe in my heart
that God will work it out for us. He has
done it before, and He will do it again.
I am still Glowing through the Map
Virus. Things haven't always been easy

or fun, but I'm still here. So many others have lost their lives, or the lives of very close loved ones. Thank God I wasn't in that number. Everyone that I know personally, who contracted the Map Virus is still here to tell their own story. To give their own testimony of God's grace and mercy that carried them through this storm. I only know who held my hand in that hospital room and walked with me all the way. Dealing with the recovery from this virus for me, or my fiancé was not going to be easy. I am just so grateful that I am still here to even do it. No more complaining. Honestly living life on life's terms was what I intend to always do being simply grateful that I am still here!!

-THE END

Made in the USA
Middletown, DE
04 July 2020